W9-BBD-223

IVy + BEAN

BOOK 9

More Praise for IVY + BEAN!

★ "Just right for kids moving on from beginning readers . . .
illustrations deftly capture the girls' personalities and the tale's
humor. . . . Barrows' narrative brims with sprightly dialogue."
—*Publishers Weekly*, starred review

★ "In the tradition of Betsy and Tacy, Ginnie and Genevra, come
two new friends, Ivy and Bean. . . . The deliciousness is in the
details here. . . . Will make readers giggle."
—*Booklist*, starred review

★ "Ivy and Bean are irresistible."
—*Kirkus Reviews*, starred review

"A charming new series." —*People*

"Ivy and Bean are a terrific buddy combo." —*Chicago Tribune*

"This is a great chapter book for students who have recently
crossed the independent reader bridge."
—*School Library Journal*

"Annie Barrows' simple and sassy text will draw in both the
reluctant reader and the young bookworm. Fans of Beverly
Cleary's Beezus and Ramona will enjoy this cleverly written and
illustrated tale of sibling rivalry and unexpected friendship."
—*BookPage*

iVy + BEAN

MAKE THE RULES

BOOK **9**

written by annie barrows + illustrated by sophie blackall

chronicle books · san francisco

To Athena, Satya, and Nike,
future Great Women of History. —A. B.

For Millie and Bella. —S. B.

This is a component of a boxed set. Not for individual retail.

Text © 2012 by Annie Barrows.
Illustrations © 2012 by Sophie Blackall.
All rights reserved. No part of this book may be reproduced in any form without written permission from the publisher.

ISBN 978-1-4521-4227-2

The Library of Congress has cataloged the original edition as follows:

Library of Congress Cataloging-in-Publication Data:
Barrows, Annie.
Ivy + Bean make the rules / written by Annie Barrows ; illustrated by Sophie Blackall.
p. cm. — (Ivy + Bean)
Summary: Seven-year-old Bean is too young to go to the camp her sister Nancy is attending, so she and her best friend Ivy decide to create their own camp.
ISBN 978-1-4521-0295-5 (alk. paper)
1. Ivy (Fictitious character : Barrows)—Juvenile fiction. 2. Bean (Fictitious character : Barrows)—Juvenile fiction. 3. Camps—Juvenile fiction. 4. Best friends—Juvenile fiction.
[1. Camps—Fiction. 2. Best friends—Fiction. 3. Friendship—Fiction.] I. Blackall, Sophie, ill.
II. Title. III. Title: Ivy and Bean make the rules. IV. Series: Barrows, Annie. Ivy + Bean ; bk. 9.

PZ7.B27576Iwbe 2012
813.6—dc23

2011051360

Manufactured in China.

MIX
Paper from responsible sources
FSC
www.fsc.org
FSC™ C020056

Series and book design by Sara Gillingham.
Typeset in Blockhead and Candida.
The illustrations in this book were rendered in Chinese ink.

2 3 4 5 LEO 17 16 15 14 13

Chronicle Books LLC
680 Second Street, San Francisco, California 94107

Chronicle Books—we see things differently.
Become part of our community at www.chroniclekids.com.

CONTENTS

NEVER 4-EVER

"Girls are strong! Girls are great!" sang Nancy, boinging into the kitchen. "Girls have the power to cre-ate!" She stomped her foot and put one arm in the air. "At GIRL POWER FOREVER!"

"Stop singing that song," said Bean grumpily. She sucked the milk out of her spoon. Then she slurped down the cereal that was left behind.

Nancy watched. "That's got to be the slowest way to eat cereal in the entire world."

"I know," said Bean, slurping. "That's why I do it. To make it last longer."

"Well, cut it out," Nancy said. "I have to get to camp. Today's the first day!"

As if Bean didn't know that already. Camp, camp, camp. Nancy had been talking about it  for weeks. And there it was, right on her T-shirt, in big letters: Girl Power 4-Ever! For spring break, Nancy was going to Girl Power 4-Ever Camp. Bean was too young for Girl Power 4-Ever Camp. You had to be eleven. If you were seven, like some people, the only camp you could go to was Puppet Fun! Bean would never in a million years go to Puppet Fun!

Nancy dropped her backpack on the kitchen table and opened one of its many pockets. Nancy's backpack was a fancy

zebra-striped kind. There was a tiny troll doll attached to one of its zippers. Bean's backpack was dirty and orange, and she had tried to draw an eagle on the front, but it hadn't turned out right. It looked like a slug with wings.

Nancy pulled out her special folding brush and brushed her already-brushed hair. Without even looking, she made a ponytail and fixed it with a sparkly scrunchie. "Hurry up," she said to Bean. "Just eat it."

Bean took a long, slow slurp. "I don't see why I have to hurry," she said. "I'm not going to your old camp."

"You can go when you're eleven," Nancy said.

Bean scowled. "No way! Camp? Ha! Not for me." She shook her head. "I've got too much other stuff to do."

Nancy smiled. "What kind of stuff?"

Bean shook her head like she had so much to do that she couldn't even begin to tell about it.

Nancy patted her shoulder sympathetically. "Finish your cereal. You have to go with Mom to drop me off at camp."

"Stop feeling sorry for me," snapped Bean. But Nancy had already left the room, her ponytail swishing, on her way to have secret, big-kid fun that Bean wasn't allowed to have. Bean pushed out her chair and stood up. "I'm not a baby, you know," she yelled.

+ + + + + +

Five million girls in pink Girl Power 4-Ever shirts were squirming around outside the Youth Center, waiting for camp to begin. They hugged each other and squealed. They showed each other their cell phones. They sang.

They danced. They
giggled. They were all
bouncy and happy and busy.

Bean stood beside her mother. Unbouncy,
unhappy, unbusy. She watched as Nancy
rushed to her friend, Didi. Once they had

hugged and squealed, they gave each other piggyback rides. Then they traded scrunchies and squealed some more. Then someone blew a whistle, and all five million girls swarmed into the Youth Center.

"Bye, Mom!" called Nancy, swinging her backpack over her shoulder. "Bye, Beanie!"

Beanie? Phooey. Bean turned and began to trudge home beside her mother. At least she didn't have to trudge far. The Youth Center was a big shed on the edge of Monkey Park, just a block and a half from Bean's house.

"What's that camp about, anyway?" Bean asked. Not that she cared.

Her mom stopped and rattled around in her purse. "I've got a brochure in here somewhere," she said. "Oh. Here it is." She pulled out a pink sheet of paper with daisies on it.

Bean read:

GIRL P✿WER
4 - EVER!

A Week of Inspiration and Fun for Girls!
Ages 11 – 14

Crafts
Nature Study
Mind/Body Strength Training
Drama
First Aid
Dance
Social Skills
Plus! Our Role Models: Great Women of History

Hands-On Learning in a Safe and Supportive
Atmosphere
(Snacks Provided.)

Her mom smiled at her. "You wish you were going to camp, too, don't you?"

Bean was getting ding-dang tired of people looking at her sympathetically. "No!" And she didn't. Not really.

"I can still get you into Puppet Fun!" her mom said.

"No!" Bean yelled. "I've got too much to do. Ivy and I have important plans for this week."

Her mother stopped walking and crouched down to look in Bean's eyes. "Okay. You're probably too grown-up for Puppet Fun! anyway. You're getting to be a pretty big kid." Bean nodded. She was. Her mom went on, "I think you might be old enough to do something new."

"You're going to get me a dirt bike?!" Bean broke in.

Her mom laughed. "No. I wasn't thinking of a dirt bike. I was thinking that maybe you are big enough to come here to Monkey Park by yourself, if you come with Ivy and if it's okay with Katrine." Katrine was Ivy's mom.

Bean sighed inside herself and turned to look at Monkey Park. Its real name was Mrs. Taylor Hopper Ansuch Memorial Park, but everybody called it Monkey Park because it had a fountain with a statue of a smiling monkey in the middle. The monkey was dressed in a shiny blue suit, and he held a big, shiny platter

of oranges and grapes. The fountain water spurted out of his hat. Besides the fountain, Monkey Park had one big flat field and one not-so-flat field and a playground filled with babies. There were some trees and some bushes and some flowers.

Kids played soccer at Monkey Park. Families had picnics there. Babies crawled up the play structure. Nothing exciting had ever happened in Monkey Park. Going to Monkey Park was the opposite of going to Girl Power 4-Ever Camp. But Bean knew her mother was trying to be nice, so she nodded. "Okay."

They walked home. As they climbed the front stairs, Bean's mom said, "You can always help with the dishes, if you're looking for something to do. Big kids help."

"Sorry," said Bean. "I'm only seven."

UN-MAGIC TREE HOUSE

Bean did have important plans. Okay, one important plan. It was about a board. She had found a good board, a really good one. It was wide and strong and smooth. It had probably been a bookshelf once, but when Bean saw it, she knew that it was meant to be a tree house. It would be the floor of Bean's tree house, her secret hideaway, her fort, her almost-apartment up in the leaves, where no one could come unless Bean gave her permission. Except Ivy, because Ivy was going to help her build it. They were going to be tree housemates.

There was one problem with Bean's plan. Trees. Bean's backyard had trees, but not trees with nice, low, friendly branches. It had trees with high, unfriendly branches. Bean had tried putting her board in a bush, but that didn't work. The bush had sort of fallen over. Bean had gritted her teeth and lugged the board to her front yard, where there was a plum tree with some sturdy branches. A front-yard tree house was not as good as a

backyard tree house, but Bean was trying to be open-minded.

Another problem was nails. Bean was not supposed to use them. Or hammers. Her dad had promised to nail the board into the plum tree, but he kept forgetting.

Now, as Bean thought about Nancy and Girl Power 4-Ever Camp, she decided she couldn't wait for her dad. She had to make her tree house today. No hammer and nails? Fine. She would find another way, a better way. Nancy would come home from camp and wish she had a tree house like Bean's. Bean might let her sit inside it for one minute.

Bean looked over at Ivy's house, on the other side of Pancake Court. The curtains were closed. But that was okay. Bean could do it on her own. "Girls are strong, girls are great," she sang softly. "Girls have the power to cre-ate."

Feeling determined, Bean set to work. The first question was how to stick things together without nails. Easy-peasy! Duct tape! Bean raced inside and came out with a thick roll of tape. She was getting more determined by the moment. Probably kids would cluster around the bottom of the plum tree, hoping to be allowed in her tree house. She shoved the board up into the tree's branches, looked at it for a second, and then went inside to get a chair. She banged her knee dragging the chair over the lawn, and it wasn't very good for the lawn, but at last she was ready. She stood on the seat, wrapping tape around the board and the branch. Tape, tape, tape. Okay! Done!

She got down and moved the chair to the other end of the board. Tape, tape, tape—

"Hi."

"Yikes!" Bean grabbed the tree to keep from falling off her chair.

"Did I scare you?" Ivy looked pleased. "I'm trying to walk without making any sound."

"Why do you want to do that?" asked Bean.

"So I can creep up on people and cast spells on them," Ivy said. Ivy was going to be a witch when she grew up, so she needed to know things like that.

"Oh. Can you hold onto this side while I tape the other end?"

Ivy stood on the chair beside Bean. Bean taped up a storm. "There!" she exclaimed. "Done!"

They both got off the chair and stood back to look. The board looked surprisingly small, there among the branches of the plum tree. In fact, it looked puny. It didn't look like a tree house. It looked like a board. With lots of tape on it.

Bean's throat got thick and hot. Big kids made tree houses all the time. They didn't have to use tape. They used nails and a hammer. They stood on ladders, not chairs.

They pounded nails while telling jokes, and their tree houses were as big as regular houses and secret, not out in front of everyone in their front yards. Big kids built things, made things, cooked things, had things, knew things. And Bean didn't. Because she was just a little kid.

Ivy watched Bean's face. "We could fix it," she said. She meant the tree house.

"No," said Bean. "I'm sick of this tree house." She kicked the plum tree. "What good is a tree house anyway? You just sit in it. It's dumb."

"Well," said Ivy, "you could eat cookies in it."

"Eating! Eating is boring," said Bean crabbily. "I want to

do things. Fun things. Like crafts and nature study."

"Crafts and nature study?" Ivy asked. "What?"

From her pocket, Bean pulled out the Girl Power 4-Ever paper and handed it to Ivy. "That's what I want to do," she said. "I want to do all that."

Ivy read the list. "Crafts. Nature Study. First Aid." She looked up at Bean and then back at the paper. "Dance, Drama, Social Skills, Great Women of History." She began to smile. "Bean! We can do all this stuff. We don't need to go to camp. We can make our own camp!"

CAMP FLAMING ARROW
HITS THE SPOT

There are certain things a camp has to have. The first thing is counselors. The people who run camps are called counselors. They make all the decisions and they are prepared for anything. Plus, everyone has to do what they say.

"Counselor Ivy," said Bean. She saluted.

"Counselor Bean," said Ivy. She saluted, too.

Bean put the ring of duct tape on her arm. If you had duct tape, you were prepared for anything. "Okay, now let's make some decisions. The first thing we have to decide is the name."

"Okay," said Ivy. "What do you want to call it?"

"Something good," said Bean.

"Right."

"Something cool," Bean said.

"Right. Cool," agreed Ivy.

"And something kind of tough-sounding," Bean went on. "Something that will make people wish they went to our camp. Like Camp Flaming Arrow." Flaming arrows were totally cool and tough. Bean had seen them in a movie. They shot through the air and whatever they hit burned to a crisp.

"Or Camp Neanderthal," said Ivy dreamily. "Neanderthals are cool and tough." Bean had never heard of Neanderthals, so Ivy explained that they were long-gone cave people who were maybe short and stumpy, but definitely brave. They clubbed saber-toothed tigers over

the head, they were
so brave.

Bean had to agree: Neanderthals
were pretty cool. They were just as cool
as flaming arrows. How could they choose
between them?

"Eenie-meenie," Ivy suggested. So they
eenie-meenied, and when flaming arrows
won, Ivy didn't even mind very much, because
Camp Flaming Arrow was such a great name.
Who wouldn't want to be in Camp Flaming
Arrow?

Another reason Ivy didn't mind very much
about eenie-meenie was that she had her own
great idea right afterward. It was about the
tent. They needed a tent. No tent, no camp.
But unfortunately, neither Ivy nor Bean had a
tent handy. Where could they get one? For a
few minutes, they were stumped. Then Ivy got

her great idea. "Hey!" she said and jumped to her feet. "My mom got new curtains!" She began to run toward her house.

Bean didn't think that was very exciting. But, as she found out when Ivy came back, the new curtains were not the exciting part. The exciting part was the old curtains. Ivy had fished them out of the garbage, four long white pieces of cloth, perfect for tent-making. She and Bean laid the cloth out on the grass and duct-taped the tops of the curtains together to make one superwide piece of white cloth. Ta-DA! Now they had a tent.

"All we have to do is throw it over that branch and Camp Flaming Arrow can begin," said Ivy, pointing to the plum tree.

"No," said Bean. "Camp Flaming Arrow isn't here."

Ivy looked confused. "Then where is it?"

"Monkey Park," said Bean firmly. "Real camps are at Monkey Park."

+ + + + + +

Bean's mom said okay. In her backpack, Bean placed a safety pin, a Santa hat with a beard attached to it, and a wolf mask left over from Halloween. She carried a big sign that said Camp Flaming Arrow in her hands, so it wouldn't get crumpled. Presto! She was ready for camp.

Ivy's mom said okay. Ivy got the tent into her backpack, but there wasn't much room for anything else. She slipped in a few Band-Aids. Better safe than sorry, just like teachers always said. At the last minute, she jammed in her magnifying glass as well. She was ready for camp.

"BYE!" they screeched to their mothers.

At the edge of the park, they stopped.

"Whoa, Nellie," Bean said. Monkey Park was bursting with kids. On the big flat field, there were two soccer games going on, with another pack of kids jumping up and down on the side. On the not-so-flat field, kids clustered around a picnic table, doing something with paper bags. A bunch more kids were having a tug-of-war with some teenagers. More kids

sat in the grass, listening
to a man talk about Indians.
Over in the playground, babies
were falling down and sliding and
screaming.

Nobody paid any attention as Bean and Ivy
walked over to the side of the park where the
trees were. They flung the two-curtain-wide
cloth over a tree branch and carefully spread
out the edges that touched the ground. They
went inside. They came back outside and put
rocks on the edges to make them stay. Bean
unrolled the Camp Flaming Arrow sign and
stuck it to the tent with her safety pin.

Ivy and Bean looked at each
other and smiled. Camp
Flaming Arrow was
open for business.

VERY CRAFTY

Bean and Ivy went inside their tent. They came out. They sat on the grass. They got up. They walked around. They sat back down again.

Finally, Ivy said, "What exactly do you do at camp?"

Bean pulled out the Girl Power 4-Ever paper and looked at the list. "All this stuff is what you do."

Ivy nodded. "But what comes first?"

"I'm not sure," said Bean. "That's why I brought these." She held up the wolf mask and the Santa hat.

"Wolf and Santa camp?" asked Ivy. "That sounds fun."

"No, we're going to go to the Youth Center and spy on Girl Power 4-Ever Camp," said Bean. She put the wolf mask over her face and handed the Santa hat and beard to Ivy. "Whatever they're doing, we'll do it too."

Ivy put on the Santa hat. Hunks of beard fell off in her mouth. "Don't you think they might notice a wolf and a Santa spying on them?"

"Nah," said Bean. "We're going to be really quiet. They won't notice a thing."

"Then why are we wearing this stuff?" asked Ivy, pulling Santa hair out of her mouth.

"Just to be on the safe side," said Bean. "Because if Nancy does notice us, she's going to lose her marbles."

+ + + + + +

Wolf eyes are not in the same place as people eyes, Bean realized. After she smacked into a tree for the second time, Bean decided to take the mask off until she got to the Youth Center. Santa didn't have a problem seeing. Santa had a problem breathing. With every breath, big puffs of beard flew into Ivy's throat and made her cough. "Shh," warned Bean.

"I can't help it," choked Ivy.

"Spit," said Bean.

So Ivy did. That helped some.

They slithered among the Monkey Park trees. Even without her mask, Bean was a wolf, hunting her prey, tiptoe, tiptoe. Ivy was Santa, trying to deliver presents without waking up all the kids, tiptoe, tiptoe. They were almost there. Bean and Ivy whisked across a patch of grass and huddled against the cement walls of the Youth Center, tiptoe, tiptoe. They curled around the building's corner, tiptoe, tiptoe. They crouched down and scuttled underneath the window, and Bean snapped her mask on. Slowly, slowly, they stood up and peeked in the window.

At long tables, rows of girls were bent over tiny threads, knotting and knotting. Ivy nudged Bean and whispered, "Crafts?"

"Friendship bracelets," Bean whispered back. She looked up and down the rows for Nancy. There she was. She was crouched over a table piled with colored threads. She was knotting like crazy. She was knotting so hard that her tongue was sticking out of her mouth.

"You want to do that?" whispered Ivy.

Bean looked at the knotters again. It was real camp. In real camp, they made friendship bracelets. "Yeah," Bean whispered.

Ivy nodded. "Okay, if you want to."

Unfortunately, nodding let loose a big fluff of beard. And very unfortunately, Ivy breathed it in and began coughing. And extra-unfortunately, three Girl Power 4-Ever campers glanced up and saw a wolf and a choking Santa peeking in the window. And then, really quite unfortunately, they screamed, "OMG! OMG! WHAT WAS THAT?" and Nancy looked up.

But fortunately, Ivy and Bean were long gone by that time. By that time, they were racing wildly through the trees, zip zip zip, tearing off the wolf mask and the Santa hat and beard. They reached Camp Flaming Arrow and flung themselves into their tent. Then they lay there, gasping.

CAMP
FLAMING
ARROW

"Time for crafts!" Bean wheezed.

+ + + + + +

Since Ivy was still choking on Santa fuzz, Bean ran to her house to get string. She came back to Camp Flaming Arrow a few minutes later holding twelve neat coils of colored string.

"Where'd you get those?" asked Ivy.

Bean said, "One of the best things about Nancy being in camp is that she isn't in her room."

"Won't she mind?"

"Nah," said Bean. "She has tons of it. She won't even notice."

"Didn't you just say that about the mask and the Santa?" asked Ivy. She looked at the strings. "How do you make a friendship bracelet, anyway?"

Bean felt like a real counselor. "The first thing you do is pick your colors," she said.

They picked their colors. The twelve neat coils of string turned into a brightly colored mound of string.

"Next, you put all six of your strings together and tie a knot," said Bean. She was pretty sure that was what you did, anyway. She looked at Ivy's knot. "Very good," she said. "Now, you make more knots, one in each string." The more knots, the better, she figured.

"More knots?" asked Ivy. Making knots took a lot of concentration.

"That's what friendship bracelets are all about. Knots," said Bean briskly. She started knotting her own strings. Knot, knot, knot. Knot. Wait. She had tied one string to another. Bummer.

"My string's all bunched up," said Ivy.

"Undo it," said Bean, trying to untie her bad knot.

"I can't," said Ivy.

Bean sliced one of her strings in half with her fingernail. Now she had seven strings. Yow. String-o-rama.

"Now my first knot's undone," Ivy announced.

"Mine turned into two strings," Bean said.

"You know," said Ivy. "I already know we're friends. It's not like I need a bracelet to figure it out."

Now three of Bean's strings were split. She had thirteen strings. "Stupid strings," she muttered. She tried to untangle them. When she looked up, she saw that Ivy had wrapped all of her strings around her own wrists. She was using her teeth to tie the ends in a knot.

"What are you doing?" Bean asked. "That's not a craft."

"I'm being Houdini," said Ivy. "No rope could hold him. He could escape from

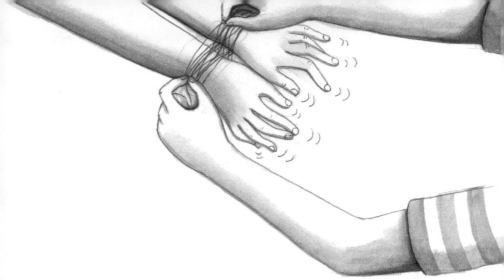

anything." She held out her wrists. "Tie this knot and I'll show you how he did it."

Bean threw her strings on the ground. "There's no way you'd escape if I tied my special knot."

"That's what you think," said Ivy. "I'm getting really good at escaping."

Bean leaned over and tied the string around Ivy's wrists, knotting once, twice, three times. "Hey!" she said. "Look! It's a friendship bracelet."

HAPPY CAMPERS

Ivy had just finished tying Bean's arm and leg together behind her back when they heard a voice say, "That's weird."

"What?" said Ivy, looking around. She got up to investigate.

"Hey!" called Bean. "You can't just walk away!"

"What are you doing?" asked Ivy.

"I'm trying to get the heck out of this rope!" yelled Bean. But Ivy was talking to someone else. Two someone elses. They were peeking out of a bush.

"We're running away from home," said one of them. He was a little kid, littler than Ivy and Bean.

"No, we're not. He says anything," the other one said. She was about their age. "Are you doing a trick?"

"Welcome to Camp Flaming Arrow," said Bean in her best counselor voice. It was hard to look like a counselor with her foot tied to her hand, but she tried.

"Camp What?" asked the girl.

"Camp Flaming Arrow," said Ivy. "You know, whoosh through the air, sizzle." She added, "Some people call it Camp Neanderthal."

The girl looked at Bean. "Why is she all tied up?"

"Crafts!" yelled Bean, struggling to get her foot free.

The boy set down his backpack. "That's a good craft. Can I be in your camp?"

"I thought you were running away from home," said Ivy.

"No." The girl shook her head. "We're visiting our great-aunt. She told us to come here and play. We can't go back to her house until dinner."

"Wow," said Ivy. "Dinner's a long time from now."

The girl nodded. "She's kind of crabby."

Bean heaved herself over onto her side with a thump. She smiled, showing all her teeth. "Welcome to Camp Flaming Arrow, a week of fun and inspiration for g—kids." The boy was a boy, so it couldn't be just for girls. "I'm Counselor Bean, and that girl is Counselor Ivy."

+ + + + + +

The boy's name was Harlan, and he was six years old. His sister was Franny, and she was seven. Harlan asked where the other campers were.

Bean tried to think of a good answer. She couldn't. "Actually, there aren't any other—"

"Camp doesn't really start until next week," Ivy broke in.

"Right!" said Bean. "This is practice week. Just for counselors."

"But we'll make an exception for you," said Ivy.

Bean nodded seriously. "You're lucky. If you came next week, you might not get in. This camp is pretty popular." Ivy nodded seriously, too.

"You don't look very old to be counselors," said Franny.

"Oh, we're old all right," said Bean.

"We're short for our ages," said Ivy. "Really short." She sighed sadly.

Harlan and Franny could tell that it wouldn't be polite to ask any more questions about that.

"Now! We always start with a little talk about camp rules!" said Bean, rubbing her hands together. "So sit down! Crisscross applesauce! Hop to it!"

Harlan and Franny plopped down on the grass and waited obediently. Ivy and Bean looked at each other with shining eyes. This was going to be good. No one ever let them make the rules.

"Rule number one!" said Bean. "You can only have as much fun as you are willing to get hurt!"

"What?" said Franny.

"Rule two!" said Ivy. "Live and learn!" Her mom said that a lot.

"Rule three!" yelled Bean. "The counselor is always right!"

Ivy began to giggle. "Rule four! If you want to make an omelet, you're going to have to break some eggs!"

"If you can't beat 'em, join 'em!" bellowed Bean.

"Don't get mad, get even!" yelled Ivy.

"I don't think this is a real camp," said Franny.

"Time for crafts!" shouted Bean.

+ + + + + +

"How was your day, Bean?" her dad asked that night at dinner.

"Great," said Bean.

"What did you do?"

"Great," said Bean. She was thinking about crafts. It had been a lot of fun. Even Franny and Harlan had had fun. They were the kind of kids who enjoyed having their hands tied to their feet.

"What?" said her dad.

Bean turned to Nancy. "How was Girl Power 4-Ever?" she asked.

"Super-duper fun!" Nancy said, shoving a forkful of pasta into her mouth.

"What exactly did you do?" asked Bean.

"Well! We did nature study first, and then—"

"What's nature study?" asked Bean.

"You know, studying nature! Duh!" said Nancy. "And then we had crafts and dance and I'm in a routine and—wait." Her eyes got narrow. "Why do you want to know?"

Bean opened her eyes wide and pitiful. "I'm just interested in your life. Isn't that all right?"

"No," said Nancy. Her eyes got even narrower. "Leave my life alone."

"Nancy," said her mother. "Don't be mean to your little sister."

"Yeah," said Bean. "I'm just a little kid."

When their parents weren't looking, Nancy stuck her tongue out at Bean.

MONKEY PARK GONE WILD

Ivy was the counselor in charge of nature study. It was only fair. She knew a lot about nature. She knew about bugs and dinosaurs and tornadoes. But what the heck was nature study? Ivy wasn't sure. So the next morning, she brought every nature-y thing she could think of to Camp Flaming Arrow.

"Please be seated," said Ivy to Harlan and Franny. They sat.

"These are our nature study materials. Our kit." That was good. A kit sounded like something a counselor would have. "This is a magnifying glass." She held it up.

"We know," said Franny.

"Shh," said Bean.

Ivy held up a pair of goggles. "These are goggles. They protect your eyes during explosions."

"Explosions?" said Harlan.

Ivy held up binoculars. "For seeing things that are far away."

"Like what?" said Franny. "What are we going to see?"

"Shh," said Bean.

"Paper bags," said Ivy, waving them. "For specimens."

"What specimens?" said Franny. "I don't see any specimens."

"Hey," said Bean. "The counselor is always right."

"I don't think this is real nature study," grumbled Franny. "Let's do more crafts, like yesterday."

Bean was just about to get mad when Ivy spoke. "Fine," she said, like she didn't care. "If you want to go off by yourself and do crafts, that's okay. But you'll be missing a very special event. A very unusual event." She smiled. "Today's nature study is," she paused dramatically, "the Komodo dragon."

"A dragon?" squeaked Harlan.

"Komodo dragons are lizards," Ivy explained. "They're longer than two grownups put together. Their spit is red and poisonous. And guess what: They don't ever poop."

"What do they look like?" asked Harlan. "How can they not poop?"

"They look like giant brown lizards," answered Ivy. "They can't chew. They don't have any taste buds." She didn't know how they could not poop, so she didn't answer that question.

"Do they live here?" asked Harlan, looking around. "How can they not poop?"

"They eat goats whole," said Ivy.

"And they live here, in Monkey Park?" asked Franny. She didn't sound like she believed it.

Ivy looked at Bean. "Komodo dragons are very, very rare in Monkey Park," she said. "But we might get lucky today." This was true. There *might* be a Komodo dragon that had escaped from the zoo. "It's just possible. In fact, I think I'd better go get my Komodo-catcher, just in case."

"Really?" said Harlan. He bounced a little. "We're going to catch one?"

"Maybe," said Ivy. "I'll be right back."

While Ivy ran to her house, Bean gave the campers a pep talk. At least, it started out as a pep talk. "Nature study is one of the most important parts of camp," she said. "But it's also the most dangerous." She squinted her eyes like a cowboy. "We've lost a few campers in nature study."

"Lost?" asked Harlan. "Where?"

Bean shook her head slowly. She was feeling more like a cowboy every minute. "Monkey Park," she drawled. "It's wild land."

Harlan looked worried. "Maybe we should skip nature study."

"It ain't camp without nature study," said Bean. She wanted to spit, but usually it dribbled down her front, so she didn't. "Don't fret, little fella. We're a-going in prepared."

"You sound like a cowboy," said Franny.

"Well, ma'am," began Bean, but just then Ivy came running back with a butterfly net in her hand.

"That's a butterfly net," said Franny.

"It's a Komodo-catcher," said Ivy.

Bean picked up a thick stick. "And this-a-here is a Komodo-whopper."

Harlan put on the goggles. "What if they eat us?" he asked.

"Oh, Harlan," said Franny. "It's just made-up. There aren't any Komodo dragons."

"Don't be so sure, Missy," said Bean, rubbing the part of her face where a beard would be. "Let's move out, nice and slow."

Ivy led them through the little woods. They wound among trees, their feet crunching quietly over leaves, and Bean began to think that if there were a Komodo dragon, it would be very hard to see.

It might creep up on them.

With its red and poisonous spit.

"Halt!" Ivy whisper-shouted. Bean and Harlan and Franny halted. Ivy bent down and scrabbled in the dirt. "Look!" She pointed. "Footprints!"

Bean leaned in and saw a big, five-toed footprint. "Komodo?" she asked.

Ivy nodded wisely. "Be very quiet," she whispered.

Hardly breathing, they
walked on. Step, step, step.

"Hark!" Ivy whispered.
"Was that the call of the Komodo dragon?"

"Who-o!" Bean said out of the side of her
mouth.

"That's you!" said Franny.

"No. That was the yellow-bellied sap-sucker," said Ivy. Suddenly, she bent and scrabbled in the dirt again. "Look!" she cried. "A specimen!" She held up a muddy lump. "The Komodo has been here."

Harlan lifted up his goggles to get a good look. "What is that thing?"

"This? This is the remains of the Komodo's breakfast." Ivy peered at it carefully. "I believe it was a goat."

"A goat?" Harlan said. "That was a goat?"

"Oh, Harlan," Franny said. "It wasn't a goat. She's just making it up."

Ivy turned a little bit red. "I am not making it up."

"Yes, you are," said Franny.

"I said I believed it was a goat. And I do."

Bean could see that Ivy was getting mad. Bean knew from experience that when Ivy got mad, she got stubborn. She could see that Franny was stubborn, too. They were probably going to have an argument. Yup, now they were having it.

"You don't know anything about Komodo dragons," Ivy was saying.

Bored, Bean sat down and looked over at the field. The soccer teams were there again. It wasn't a game, with moms and dads watching. It was a bunch of kids kicking a ball around while a teenager yelled at them. Soccer camp, Bean guessed. Hey, one of the kids was Leo, who went to school with Ivy and Bean. He was mostly their friend, even though he called them wackos sometimes.

As Bean watched, the teenager stopped yelling and walked away, talking on his cell phone. As soon as his back was turned, the soccer kids went bonkers, kicking balls this way and that. "Goal! Goal! Goooal!" they screamed, racing around the field. Leo was one of the fastest, zigzagging and screeching and waving his arms wildly.

Wildly.

Bean started to laugh. "Hey!" She poked Ivy with her stick. "Check it out! An escaped Komodo dragon!" She pointed at Leo.

"What?" said Franny.

Ivy turned and saw. She giggled. "Wow. A whole herd of them."

"Get the big one!" yelled Bean. She jumped up and began to run, waving her whopper. Ivy followed with her butterfly net. "Komodo hunt!" Bean screamed to Franny and Harlan, and they took off behind her.

Leo was so busy zipping around that he didn't notice Bean until she was right next to him. "Hey!" he said. "Bean! What're you doing?"

"Get him!" she yelled to Ivy.

Ivy almost got the net over Leo's head, but he dodged away.

"Head him off at the pass!" cried Bean to Harlan and Franny.

Leo didn't bother asking any more questions after that. He just ran.

Waggling the whopper over her head, Bean charged after him. "Circle around! Circle around!" she shrieked. Leo looked over his shoulder and headed for the trees. Ivy and Franny and Harlan tore after him. He swung around and headed in the other direction, but there was Bean and her whopper. Leo turned again, and ran smack into Ivy.

"Got him!" Ivy yelled, which wasn't exactly true, since she and Leo were both on the ground.

"Bag him!" hollered Bean, and Ivy dropped the net over Leo's head. "Good work," panted Bean, galloping up with Harlan and Franny.

Leo was panting, too. "What are"—pant, pant—"you guys doing?"

Bean poked Leo with her whopper. "I'll be goll-blamed. It's a talking Komodo!"

"Very rare," gasped Ivy.

Leo looked at them. "What are you guys talking about?"

"You're a Komodo dragon," Harlan said.

"A small one," said Bean.

"A runt," giggled Ivy.

"I am not!" said Leo. "Come on. What is this?"

"It's a camp," said Ivy.

"We're the counselors," explained Bean.

"This is nature study," said Franny.

"A Komodo dragon hunt," said Ivy.

"And you're the Komodo dragon," Harlan told him.

Leo took the net off his head. "You guys are wackos, you know that?"

Bean stood up. "Come on, little campers, let's move out."

"Wait!" Leo said. He

rolled over on his stomach. "You want to hunt a real Komodo dragon? Try catching that kid over there." He pointed at a kid who was whizzing by with a soccer ball. "Hey! Juanito! You're a Komodo!" Leo yelled.

The kid stopped whizzing. "What?"

"Get him!"

TAPPETTYTAPTAP!

That night, Nancy talked about her routine. A lot.

"But what is it?" Bean asked.

"You know. A dance. To a song. Like a music video," said Nancy.

"Hello? I'm not allowed to watch music videos," said Bean.

Nancy rolled her eyes. "Okay," she said. "I'll show you." She hopped up from her chair and twirled around. "And then we go like this." She walked sideways, to the right, to the left. "Then, watch this." She swung her hands up in the air and looked at them. "That's the best part," she said.

Bean wondered how that could be the best part. "Is that it?" she asked.

"Yeah," said Nancy.

It was the most boring dance Bean had ever seen, but she didn't say that. "Great," she said. "That was really great."

"Thanks!" said Nancy. "Isn't the arm part good?"

"Yeah," said Bean, trying to sound enthusiastic. "Really good arm part. So—did you do anything else in camp today, anything besides the routine?"

"First we had to decide what to wear for the routine . . . "

Bean stopped listening. Dance. She could do a dance, and her dance wouldn't be boring. Her dance would be good. She had everything she needed for a good dance, right in her basement.

+ + + + + +

There were many interesting things in Bean's basement, and one of them was a metal washtub. Bean's mom had bobbed for apples in it when she was a kid. It was big, but it wasn't so big that Bean couldn't carry it. And that was good, because the next morning, she carried it all the way to Monkey Park.

Harlan and Franny were already there. "What's that?" Harlan yelled.

Bean plunked down the tub. "What are you doing here this early?"

"Aunt Eartha kicked us out," said Harlan.

"Harlan told her about Komodo dragons, and she got all mad," said Franny.

"I think it was the poop," explained Harlan.

Juanito poked his head out of the tent. "Hi."

"Hey, what are you doing here?" asked Bean.

"Hiding from Coach," said Juanito. "Are we going to do that dragon thing again?"

"No," said Bean. "Today is something different. We'll start as soon as Ivy gets here."

Ivy came, and Leo, too. "Today, campers," said Bean, "we will be learning to dance."

"Ew," said Leo. "No way."

"I'm outta here," said Juanito. He started walking away.

Bean held out her hand. "Thumbtacks, please, Counselor Ivy."

Leo and Juanito stopped walking. Thumbtacks?

"Now. First, you have to have *really* thick-bottomed shoes." Bean checked her campers' shoes. "Excellent. Second, you stick six thumbtacks in the bottom of each shoe. I will demonstrate." Bean felt just like her teacher, Ms. Aruba-Tate, as she bent down and stuck six thumbtacks into the bottom of each shoe.

"And now, we dance," she said. Harlan and Franny clapped. Leo and Juanito moved a little closer.

Bean bowed and stepped onto the top of the tub. She tapped one foot. Then the other. Good noise.

She tappety-tapped. Tappety-tap, tap, tap, ataptaptaptaptapTAPTAPTAPTAP!

The noise was nice and loud. TAPPETY-TAPPETYTAPPETYARAPTAP**TAP**!

The noise was astounding. Leo and Juanito came back.

"Isn't this great?" yelled Bean over her tapping.

"Let me try!" Franny cried. She and Harlan put thumbtacks in their shoes and danced together on the tub, making a truly incredible amount of noise. Dogs barked. Passing cars slowed. All the other camps stopped to watch.

Pretty soon, Bean, Franny, Harlan, Leo, and Juanito were crammed onto the tub, dancing their hearts out. Ivy was trying to explain to their friend Sophie W. and a kid named Ella that they'd get their turn next. A counselor was trying to get Ella to come back to Puppet Fun! No one could hear a thing.

+ + + + + +

Late in the afternoon, Bean lay in the grass in front of the tent. She was happy. Dance had been great. Well, dance had been great until Bean's mom came to the park and took the tub away. She said she could hear it all the way at Bean's house. "Don't you like the sound of dancing children?" asked Bean.

"No," her mom had said.

Juanito and Leo's coach made them go to soccer camp, but they'd come back later, for strength training. Leo and Juanito knew

all about strength training. You had to start easy. Camp Flaming Arrow had started with a grape. Picking up a grape is easy. After the grape, the campers went on to heavier things, like rocks and Harlan. Leo said he could pick up a car, but then he wouldn't show them, so no one believed him. Ella, who had tunneled out under the picnic table of Puppet Fun!, said that she could pick up her dad, but no one believed her either. Sophie W. said if they all stuck two fingers under Ivy and thought about water, they'd be able to lift her. They did that until Harlan forgot to think about water and Ivy hurt her head.

"Camp Flaming Arrow is getting big," said Ivy. She was lying on the grass too. "We've got six campers now."

"That's because it's such a great camp," said Bean.

ZOMBIE PROBLEM IN MONKEY PARK

On Thursday, Camp Flaming Arrow got even bigger. Dino from Pancake Court came with Sophie W. He was supposed to be in Animal Adventures Camp, but Animal Adventures Camp had turned out to be going to the zoo. He had already been to the zoo three times that week, and he was tired of it.

"I don't want to do anything with animals," said Dino. "I don't even want to think about an animal."

"You might have to think about Komodo dragons," called Juanito from inside the tent. He was hiding from his coach again.

"They don't poop!" yelled Harlan.

"Enough chitchat!" said Bean, just like a real counselor. "No animals. Today we will be studying first aid." First aid was on the Girl Power 4-Ever list. "And here is Counselor Ivy, to teach you important first aid tips."

First aid was fun. Ivy had brought her face paint, and they used up almost all the red. Red was the blood.

She had brought another old curtain, cut up. Those were the bandages. All the campers needed lots of bandages.

"I think he'd better take some CPR," said Bean the doctor. "His condition is serious."

Harlan groaned. He was a very good groaner.

"One-twelve over five in the plexer-carpaloo," said Franny. She gave Harlan a fake shot. He groaned.

By the time Leo got away from soccer camp, they were all covered with fake blood and bandages. He told them about a kind of first aid called the Heimlich Maneuver. When someone was choking, you pounded his stomach in just the right way, and whatever was choking him flew out of his mouth and landed across the room. That was fun. Disgusting, but fun.

They played Heimlich Maneuver for a long time, and then Dino had a great idea. Since they were already covered in fake blood, they could be zombies. They zombied around Monkey Park with their arms stretched out in front of them. By mistake, they zombied right through Puppet Fun!

"Now, boys and girls, we pull the yarn with our special needle, very, very carefully through the paper," the counselor was saying.

"UUNNN-huh!" moaned Bean the zombie.

"Hey!" said the counselor.

"Oops," said Bean, unzombieing. "Sorry."

But it was too late. Most of the Puppet Fun! campers turned into zombies on the spot.

"Now stop that!" said the counselor. "This is Puppet Fun!"

"Sorry!" said Bean. She backed toward Camp Flaming Arrow, but three new zombies

ran after her. By four o'clock in the afternoon, Monkey Park had a real zombie problem.

+ + + + + +

"We haven't done great women of history," whispered Bean into the phone that night. She was reading the Girl Power 4-Ever paper.

"Is that the only one we haven't done?" whispered Ivy, even though she didn't live with Nancy so there was no reason for her to whisper.

"There's drama, but I think being zombies could count as drama, don't you?" Bean said. "And I still don't know what a social skill is."

"It's not in the dictionary," Ivy said. "I looked it up."

"That leaves great women of history. What do you think it is?"

"I have a book about great women of history," Ivy said. "I'll bring it tomorrow."

"Mom!" hollered Nancy.

"Got to go!" whispered Bean. She stuffed the paper in her pocket just as Nancy thumped into the kitchen.

"What?" said Bean's mom, looking up from her book.

"Tell me the truth," said Nancy. "Do I look okay?"

"Sure," said Bean's mom. "You look cute."

"You don't notice anything?" Nancy asked.

Bean's mom looked at Nancy carefully. "Um. No."

"Bean?" Nancy asked. "Do you?"

"You've got a wart on your knuckle," Bean said.

Nancy shrieked, "Oh no, oh no! It's totally ugly! I'm, like, diseased!"

Bean's mom quickly put her arms around Nancy. "Honey! Nobody's going to notice a tiny little wart."

"Bean noticed!" Nancy moaned.

"You told me to look!" said Bean. Sheesh.

"I can't get up and dance with a wart," wailed Nancy. "Everyone will think I'm gross!" She ran out of the kitchen. She was crying.

Bean's mother sighed. She looked over at Bean, and then she followed Nancy.

Bean watched her go, frowning. What was that all about?

THE QUEEN'S GARBAGE

The last day of Camp Flaming Arrow started out quietly. In front of the tent, Harlan and Franny and Dino and Sophie W. gathered around Ivy and Bean. Juanito and Leo were hiding inside the tent. The Puppet Fun! counselor had given up on Ella and the three zombies as long as they promised to stay in Monkey Park, so they were there, too. Everyone was listening to Ivy.

Ivy was going to read from a book called *Daredevils in Dresses: Heroines of History*. "Boudicca, Queen of the Britons," Ivy read. She looked up. "Boudicca had red hair, like me."

Boudicca, it turned out, was a tough patootie who had lived a long time ago. When her husband died, she was supposed to get his kingdom, but the rotten Roman governor said ha, ha, I'm the governor and I get what I want. He took her kingdom and he even threw her in jail. But then he made a big mistake. He went on vacation.

Boudicca escaped from jail and told all the men in her kingdom to get off their duffs and fight for her. But they said no. They were wimps. Boudicca said fine, I'll do it myself, and she led an army from her chariot. A chariot is a bitty carriage pulled by horses. Boudicca swung her sword left and right and mowed down all the Romans in sight. There was a very interesting picture of that in the book. "And when the governor heard that Boudicca was coming in her chariot, he and his army ran away," read Ivy. "With their knees quaking in terror."

"Quaking in terror," Bean repeated. Boudicca was brave. Boudicca was cool.

There was a silence while they all thought about Boudicca.

"Now," said Ivy, putting the book down, "it's time for hands-on learning."

Bean nodded like she knew what that was. Maybe someone else would ask.

"Hands-on what?" said Dino.

"Hands-on learning means I get to be Boudicca first, because I have red hair," said Ivy. "Bean's my sister. You guys," she pointed at Sophie W., Dino, Ella, and the zombies, "you're the Roman Army. The rest of you," she waved her hand, "are the Briton warriors."

+ + + + + +

The Roman Army slept peacefully on the grass. Little did they know that Queen Boudicca, her sister Bean, and the Briton warriors were creeping up on them.

They didn't know it until Bean leaped out from behind a bush, screeching "Surrender, Roman dogs!"

Two of the zombies caved at once, but Dino, Sophie W., and Ella put up a good fight. In fact, they chased Harlan around until he surrendered, which was not what was supposed to happen. They put him in jail, but he was bravely rescued by Queen Boudicca and her sister, who duked it out, stick to stick, with Dino and Ella. Juanito double-crossed the queen by switching sides halfway through, but then Leo caught him and put him in chains, which was okay because the chains were really jackets. The two zombies decided they wanted to be Briton warriors

instead of Roman soldiers. Bean couldn't remember if Franny was on her side or not.

"TIME OUT!" she shouted.

Everyone stopped.

"This is too confusing. Let's all be Briton warriors," she said.

"But who's going to be the Roman Army?" asked Dino.

Bean looked at the Monkey Park lawn. "Garbage. The Roman Army is going to be garbage."

Garbage made a good army. It was good because there was plenty of garbage in Monkey Park. It was also good because they could poke holes in garbage and they couldn't poke holes in each other. When the wind began to blow the garbage around, it got even better. Those rotten Romans were trying to escape! Bean chased a coffee-cup Roman between the bushes, trying to spear it with her sword. It tumbled off, and she went after it, leaving the rest of the Britons behind.

Every time she thought she had that Roman, it rolled a little farther.

It rolled and tumbled all the way to the Youth Center. Bean stopped. Real camp. She could hear music coming from inside.

Bean circled past the window where she and Ivy had watched the Girl Power 4-Ever craft time and came to a door. She went in. The music was louder inside. It was so loud that nobody even looked her way. Bean stood at the back of the Youth Center and watched some girls walk to the right. Then they walked to the left. Then they swung their hands up in

the air and looked at them.

All the girls were dressed in black, so it was hard to tell one from the other. Bean squinted. Oh. There was Nancy. Her head was tilted up. She was looking at her hand. She wasn't smiling. She was counting. Bean could see her lips moving: "One, two, three, four; one, two, three, four." All the girls were counting. In a line, they moved forward and twirled, and then moved back.

Bean looked at the girls in the audience. They were all sitting quietly in rows. This was real camp. It looked terrible.

There was a big wail, and the music ended. The routine dancers stopped moving and stood in a line. The girls in rows began to clap nicely.

Bean stuffed her stick under her arm and began to clap. "YAYY! WAY TO GO, NANCY!" she hollered. "YAYY!"

Oops. Everyone was turning around to look at her. Even the dancers were looking at her. Nancy was looking at her.

Bean stopped yelling. There was a long silence. Yikes. How embarrassing. "Bye!" Bean called and zipped out the door before Nancy could begin freaking out.

Outside, Bean ran. That felt good. She ran back to the middle of Monkey Park, where no one was sitting still. Boudicca's army had grown. Kids were running around, chasing garbage and yelling, "Surrender, Roman dog!" Bean found Queen Boudicca running after a brown paper bag that bounced and blew over the grass.

"Hail, sister!" cried Ivy.

"To arms!" yelled Bean.

They chased the brown paper bag Roman all the way to Monkey Fountain, where—hooray!—it blew right into the water!

Queen Boudicca held up her sword and yelled, "Onward, warriors!" So they both took off their shoes and charged into the fountain. They chased that brown paper Roman around and around the monkey, sploshing and splashing. Pretty soon half of the Briton warriors were in the fountain too. A bunch of tiny kids standing beside the fountain got confused and threw more garbage into the water, but Boudicca's army fought bravely on.

"Surrender!" hollered Ivy, spearing the last candy wrapper with her stick.

"Long live the queen!" yelled Franny.

"Yah! Yah!" squalled the tiny kids.

Their squalling made all their moms look up, and once those moms looked up, they started losing their minds. Something about sticks poking eyes. In no time at all, Boudicca's warriors were kicked out of the fountain.

"I guess we'd better quit," said Bean, squeezing out her shirt.

Ivy nodded, dumping the last of the Romans into the garbage can.

"This was the best day yet," said Leo.

4-EVER AFTER

Camp Flaming Arrow was over. Harlan and Franny had been the last to go. Their dad was coming to pick them up the next day.

"I'm going to ask him if we can come next year," Harlan said.

"But this isn't a real camp," Franny said. "Is it?"

Bean tried to look mysterious. "Time will tell."

After they had said good-bye, Bean turned to the tent. "I guess we'd better take this thing down now."

"Guess so," said Ivy. She pulled on a curtain.

Nancy was lying inside.

Bean stared. "What the heck are you doing?"

"You spied on me, so I spied on you," said Nancy.

"I wasn't spying on you," Bean said. "I was just sort of watching."

"Did you like our routine?" asked Nancy.

"It was great!" lied Bean. "It looked super-fun."

Nancy sighed. "Actually, it was kind of boring."

"Yeah," agreed Bean.

Nancy sighed again. "I thought it was going to be fun. But then it was just the same thing over and over," she said.

"Couldn't you quit?" asked Ivy. "I would have quit."

"Nope," said Nancy. "Once you started, you had to finish. That was the rule."

"That's a terrible rule," said Bean.

"Our camp didn't have rules like that," said Ivy.

Nancy smiled. "You guys had a pretend camp?"

"It wasn't pretend!" Ivy said.

"Whatever," said Nancy. She looked at Ivy's dress. "How'd you get all wet?"

"I was Boudicca, Queen of the Britons," said Ivy proudly. "A Great Woman of History."

"You had Great Women of History?" said Nancy, surprised. "So did we!"

"We fell in Monkey Fountain," Bean said. "Boudicca's whole army fell in."

"We just had a slide show," said Nancy.

"Slide shows and rules," said Bean. "Sounds like school."

"It was kind of like school," said Nancy. "Do this, do that."

"Yuck," said Ivy.

Nancy looked between Ivy and Bean. "Was it just the two of you in your camp?"

"No. There were lots of kids here," said Ivy. "We were the counselors."

"We sort of followed this," said Bean, taking out the Girl Power 4-Ever brochure. "We were trying to be like Girl Power 4-Ever."

Nancy sneered. "I don't think so."

"We did all the same stuff!" said Bean. "We did crafts and nature study and first aid!"

"What crafts did you do?" asked Nancy.

"Friendship bracelets," Bean said. "That's how we started, anyway."

"But we ended up learning how to escape from ropes," Ivy went on. "Like Houdini."

Nancy burst out laughing. "You goons."

"We're not goons!" said Bean. "It was fun!"

"You want us to show you?" asked Ivy. "We can show you how to do it."

At first Nancy said no, but then, after a minute, she said, "Okay. Show me."

Together Ivy and Bean tied Nancy up tight, and then they told her how to get free. Nancy grunted and wiggled and laughed at them, but she was having fun, Bean could tell. After that, they showed her the Heimlich Maneuver. They described the Komodo dragon. They did strength training and how to be a zombie.

Finally, it was time to go home for dinner. Ivy folded the tent and Bean took the sign. "Camp Flaming Arrow," Nancy read aloud. "Pretty good. You guys could make a real camp. All you'd have to do is send out a brochure and make some T-shirts and stuff. I bet you'd get lots of kids signing up."

Ivy and Bean looked at each other.

Brochures? T-shirts? Sign-ups? They shook their heads. "Nah," they said together.

The End.

SNEAK PREVIEW OF BOOK 10
IVY + BEAN
TAKE THE CASE

Bean wasn't allowed to watch television. Or music videos. Bean's mom said she could watch two movies a week, but they had to be movies where everyone was good. There couldn't be any bad words. There couldn't be any mean people. There couldn't be anyone smoking a cigarette or wearing tiny clothes. There were only about ten movies that followed all these rules. Luckily, Bean liked all ten of them. She watched them over and over.

Bean's mom said ten movies were plenty. She said kids Bean's age should be using their imaginations instead of watching TV. She said fresh air was more important than movies.

And then what did she do?

She made Bean watch a movie. It was her favorite movie, she said. Everyone should see it at least once, she said. The movie was called *Seven Falls,* but it wasn't about waterfalls or even the leaf-falling kind of fall, which is what Bean had guessed. It was about a guy named Al Seven. Boy, was he tough! He was so tough he talked without moving his lips, and some of it was bad words. He was also kind of mean. Everyone in the movie was kind of mean, plus they all smoked cigarettes. They didn't wear tiny clothes, but that was the only rule they didn't break.

"I can't believe you're letting me watch this," said Bean.

"*Seven Falls* is a classic," said Bean's mom. "It's one of the greatest movies ever made."

"Don't be a stooge," said Al Seven to another movie guy. That was pretty mean, but Bean pretended not to notice, because this was one of the greatest movies ever made. Al Seven was also in black and white, but Bean knew she was supposed to imagine he was in color. "What is it about dames?" asked Al Seven, walking slowly down a rainy street. "They break your heart, I guess," he answered himself.

That was the end.

Bean's mom let out a big, happy sigh. "Wasn't that amazing? Did you get it?"

Get what? Bean wasn't sure, but she nodded. "I'm going to be just like Al Seven when I grow up."

Her mother raised one eyebrow. "You'd better not be."

But then again, why wait, thought Bean. She could start being like Al Seven now. She slumped over and put her feet on the coffee table. "Whaddaya say we watch it again, pal?" she said.

Her mom raised both eyebrows. "What I say is don't call me pal and take your feet off the table."

That hadn't worked. Bean took her feet off the table. "Dames," she said sadly. "They break your heart."

Her mom's eyebrows were almost inside her hair. "Oh dear," she said.

It took Bean a long time to go to sleep that night. She couldn't stop thinking about Al Seven and his black-and-white world. It didn't seem like the real world, the world on Pancake Court that Bean lived in. People in

Al Seven's world were tough, and they didn't laugh very much. They didn't do normal stuff like go to school and the grocery store. They walked down alleys and wore hats. But the most un-normal thing about Al Seven's world was the mysteries. There were mysteries all over the place.

Bean untwisted her pajamas and thought about that. A mystery was a question you couldn't find the answer to. In Al Seven's world, the mysteries were things like "Who took Hester's jewels?" Or "Where was Sammy La Barba on the night of May twelfth?" Bean didn't have any jewels and she sure as heck didn't know anyone named Sammy La Barba, but there were plenty of questions that she didn't have answers to. Millions of them. For instance, Who thought of money? Not even grown-ups knew the answer to that question.

But Bean had other questions, too, like What's inside the cement thing in the front yard? What's behind the Tengs' fence, and why do they lock it up? and What's the matter with the mailman? When she asked these questions, her parents usually said something like It's none of your business. That meant that there was an answer, but they didn't want her to know it.

Bean smiled toughly at her dark ceiling. They didn't want her to know things. Just like Sammy La Barba didn't want Al Seven to know where he was on the night of May twelfth. But Al Seven had figured it out, because he was a private investigator. Private investigators got to the bottom of mysteries. They solved them. They snuck around. They spied. They asked the hard questions. They sat in their cars and rubbed their faces until they came up with the answers. Then they walked down alleys in the rain.

That's what Bean was going to do. First thing tomorrow morning. "None of your business!" she muttered. "Ha!"

Now that you've read *Ivy and Bean Make the Rules*, maybe you want to make your own camp.

No Problem! Easy-peasy!

Here is a very nice list of the things you need to do.

★ DAY ONE:

1. **Pick a counselor.** That's easy: You're the counselor.
2. **Pick a name.** This is pretty easy, too. Think of something interesting, like squids, cement, bobcats, feathers, the inside of drains, your appendix (why?), jam, thermometers, freeze-tag, nests, newts, coal, dust, ants, why on earth people have five toes, wormholes, ice, whether or not you can see colors with your eyes closed, or fur. Okay! Got something good? I bet you do. That can be your camp name.
3. **Make a tent.** A tent can be just a blanket over the end of a table. A tent can be a hidey-hole inside a closet. It doesn't have to be a real tent.
4. **Get some campers.** They can be imaginary.
5. **Make some rules.** Or don't. Either way is fine!

Good work! You did it! You have a camp!

Whew, that is enough for one day. You must be tired. Go home and have a rest.

★ DAY TWO:

1. **It's fun to have a camp song. Make one up.** The tune of "America the Beautiful" is good, but then again, so is "Paint It Black." Here is the song for Camp Flaming Arrow:

> We lift our voice in grateful song
> > *Grateful song*
> We hope that you will sing along
> > *Sing along*
> For Flaming Arrow we hold so dear
> > *Hold so dear*
> Which fills our enemies with fear
> > *With fear*
> Like zombies, dread undead and mean
> > *Meeean*
> And dancing with six thumbtacks keen
> > *Very keen*
> First aid and crafts and nature's tools
> > *Nature's tools*
> And best of all: We Make the Rules!
> > *We Make the Rules!*

2. **Today is Crafts Day.** Here's a secret: Everything is a craft. Everything! Smearing peanut butter on a cracker is a craft! Juggling fruit is a craft! Wrapping yourself in paper bags is a craft! But if you want to have something that looks like a craft, try:

    FRIENDSHIP HANDCUFFS: Friendship bracelets are too complicated. All those teeny-weeny strings get tangled up and then you have to untangle them and then they break anyway. Friendship handcuffs are much better. Take as many pieces of colored string or yarn as you can get and wrap them around and around your friend's wrists. Pretty tight, but not so tight your friend's hands turn blue. Tie the best knot you can. Tie it again. Tie it another five or six times. Now tell your friend to escape from the handcuffs. Can she? If she can, tie her hand and her foot together and see if she can escape from that. Bet she can't.

Wow. What a great craft. Now go and practice whistling for a while.

 DAY THREE:

1. **Today is Nature Study.** You can put your face very, very close to the ground and think about ants. How would it feel to be one? What would you look like to an ant? Would it be a good life to be an ant? These are some very interesting questions. And then, if you want more Nature Study, you can always try:

   FIND THE NEANDERTHAL: Neanderthals lived a long time ago, and they looked mostly like people today, except they were shorter, they thumped around more when they walked, and they fought saber-toothed tigers with spears. They were probably not as smart as we are, but they were plenty brave and tough. They lived all over the place, and then for some reason they died out. At least, that's what scientists say. But how could they die out completely? There were so many of them! There's sure to be one or two Neanderthals left. Get out your butterfly net and see if you can find one. If you can't, one camper can pretend to be a Neanderthal and all the other campers can chase him or her around. That's fun, too.

★ DAY FOUR:

1. **Today is Dance.** Most dancing has a lot of rules in it. Put your arm here. Put your toe there. Phooey. Your dance doesn't have to be about rules. Your dance can be about noise.

   TAPPETY-TAP-TAP! To do this, you've got to be wearing really thick-bottom shoes, like running shoes or clogs. Are you? Okay. Good. Now, get six thumbtacks and stick them in the bottoms of your shoes, not all in one place and be careful not to stick yourself instead. Got them in there? Okay. Good. Now, get a board (or a metal washtub, but that's hard to find). Got it? Okay. Good. Now, dance. Ahahahahaha! Isn't that great?

★ ★ ★

Well, you had a camp, and it was fun. Give your counselor a pat on the back. Eat up any leftover snacks. Put the tent away. Camp is closed until next year (or next week or maybe tomorrow).

IVY+BEAN MAKE THE RULES
WORD FIND

Treasure hunt! See if you can find all the words hidden in the puzzle below.

```
S E I D U T S E R U T A N B R
F M O Q H T Z F V V W G J N J
G S W V D E H H N N U J A N K
Y F R I E N D S H I P E P S G
A V N F G T E M C M B U O E M
Y H G V D S U E C N A D F R S
H S S J O Y I Z F W U M Q O T
N B Y P F J E D R A M A P M F
T W O R R A G N I M A L F S A
T C Y P N J L H F V R O H R R
K P C O U T D O O R S F R R C
Q N E A N D E R T H A L S D T
Q V N G B Y V I F D E Q O Q A
H D I A T S R I F K B K X U L
D S J B H B I I C A M P H T A
```

WORD BANK

★ Ivy
★ Bean
★ friendship
★ Neanderthals

★ tents
★ nature studies
★ crafts
★ first aid
★ dance

★ drama
★ camp
★ flaming arrow
★ smores
★ outdoors

IVY+BEAN
CROSSWORD PUZZLE

How well do you know Ivy and Bean? Test your skills on the crossword puzzle below!

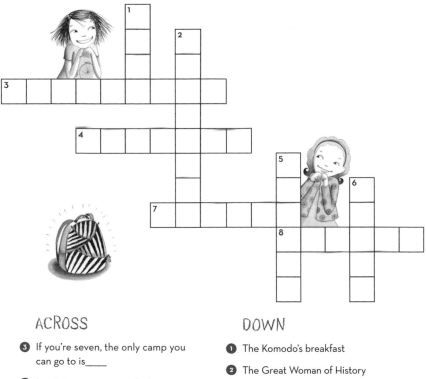

ACROSS

3 If you're seven, the only camp you can go to is_____

4 Leo is in soccer camp. So is_____

7 Camp Flaming Arrow's boy camper

8 The kind of dragon the campers were hunting

DOWN

1 The Komodo's breakfast

2 The Great Woman of History

5 Camp Flaming Arrow was at_____Park

6 Nancy's backpack has a_____doll on it

FOLLOW IVY + BEAN ON ALL OF THEIR ADVENTURES!

Collect them all. How many have you read?

BOOK ①

BOOK ②

BOOK ③

BOOK ④

BOOK ⑤

BOOK ⑥

BOOK ⑦

BOOK ⑧

BOOK ⑨

BOOK ⑩

Available wherever books are sold.

Visit **CHRONICLEBOOKS.COM/IVYANDBEAN**
for fun games, videos, and more!

HAVE EVEN MORE FUN
WITH IVY + BEAN!

Make your own buttons!

Create your own Ivy + Bean adventures with paper dolls!

More than 90 removable stickers!

Send secret notes to your friends!

Includes fold-and-seal notes and stickers!